TOWSER
and Sadie's Birthday

Tony Ross

Andersen Press · London
Hutchinson of Australia

© 1984 by Tony Ross. First published in Great Britain in ____
19–21 Conway Street, London W.1. Publishe____
Hutchinson Group (Australia) Pty. Ltd., Richm____
All rights reserved. Printed in Great ____
W.S. Cowell Ltd., Ipswich

ISBN 0 86264 049 0

"You don't look very happy this evening," said Towser to Sadie.

"It's my birthday tomorrow," she sighed.

"*That's* not so bad," laughed Towser. "Just think of all the presents you'll get."

A big tear splashed on to Sadie's armchair.

"I'll not get any," she sniffed. "I didn't last year, or the year before, or the year before that."

"I'll get you one!" said Towser grandly. "Anything you like."

Sadie brightened up like magic. "I'll have that, then," she said, pointing out of the window.

"What? A *window*!" gasped Towser.

"*No*, silly, *that*!" Sadie was pointing at the moon.

Towser gulped. "I'm not sure I can get that," he muttered.

"Oh, *I'm* sure you can do absolutely *anything*," purred Sadie, skipping away to dream of her present.

Towser went outside to study the moon. It seemed quite high up. He walked round in a circle, then made a little jump, but he couldn't reach the moon.

He scratched his nose, and picked up a longish stick. "Perhaps this'll reach it," he growled.

It didn't.

Ideas took a long time to sink into Towser's head but when they did they were usually good ideas.

"I need to be higher up!" was his good idea.

Towser climbed to the top of a nearby hill and tried again. Even with his stick, the moon was still too far away. Towser swished his stick this way and that, but the moon just smiled at him.

Towser sat down and thought the thing out. After a while he came up with a solution.

"I must get higher still!"

It was obvious really. He didn't know why he hadn't thought of it before.

He ran indoors and ran out again with some things to stand on. High things. . .

... but wobbly things.

Towser built a wobbly pile of high things, then climbed to the top of it.

Then he climbed down again, because he had forgotten his longish stick.

He wobbled to the top of his wobbly pile again and reached out with his stick.

Wobble. "... Nearly got it that – ooh..."

Wobble.

Towser strained up on tiptoe, just a little too far. His pile of high things gave one last wobble, and the whole lot came crashing down.

Towser landed on his head, which luckily was quite hard. He glared at the moon, which just seemed to smile back. Then he had another idea.

Towser rushed indoors, straight to his playroom. He flung himself into his toybox and flung his toys out. There at the bottom of the toybox was what he was looking for – a big, white balloon.

"She'll not know the difference," thought Towser, as he blew up the balloon. "It looks *just* like the moon." He felt quite the clever dog.

The white balloon got bigger and bigger until Towser thought it looked exactly the same size as the moon. Then he tied a knot in the nozzle.

Sadie was doing a spot of gardening when Towser arrived with his present.

"Happy birthday, Sadie," he said. "Here's your present – just what you wanted."

Sadie examined the balloon. "Is it the *moon*?" she gasped.

Towser nodded. He couldn't quite say, "Yes."

"It's *lovely*!" squealed Sadie.

Towser smiled.

Sadie took her moon everywhere with her. She was so happy.

"It smells a bit of rubber," she said.

"Moons do," answered Towser. "Thought *everyone* knew that!"

"I forgot," said Sadie.

Later, she said, "If you rub it, it squeaks."

"Moons often make rude noises," answered Towser. "It's to do with the cosmos."

"Cats don't know about the cosmos," said Sadie, hugging her moon.

That night, Sadie and Towser were walking in the garden and they stopped to admire the sky.

Sadie stared for a while, then pointed upwards. "Towser," she said. "If *this* is the moon, what's *that*?"

She was pointing at the real moon.

"That's the hole in the sky where the moon *was*," said Towser.

"Oh!" said Sadie, nodding.

The next day, the Wizard visited Sadie, just in case there was any birthday cake left.

"Why are you holding a saggy old balloon?" he asked.

"*Ssssh*! Not so loud," hissed Sadie. "Towser may hear. He gave it to me for my birthday. *He thinks it's the moon*. He'd be so upset if he found out it's only a balloon. Anyway, I love it awfully much."

"Isn't Sadie *nice*," thought the Wizard.

British Library Cataloguing in Publication Data
Ross, Tony
  Towser and Sadie's birthday.
  I. Title
  823′.914[J]   PZ7

ISBN 0-86264-049-0